BEFORE the ASHES

DL GALLIE

Edited by **Karen Hrdlicka**, **Barren Acres Editing** and **Tori Ellis, Cruel Ink Editing & Design**

Proofread by **Tori Ellis, Cruel Ink Editing & Design, Margaret Neal** and **Lana Clark**

Cover by **Amanda Walker PA & Design Services**

Formatting and interior design by **DL Gallie**

Coming from a long line of firefighters, I'm no stranger to flames. When Kip Kitson comes into the picture though, he sparks a fire I'm not sure how to put out.

He's the perfect package: tall, muscular, and Australian with an accent to die for.

After a single night together, we decide to take a chance and explore what could be. It's a complete whirlwind of sweet words, delicate touches, and one steamy amazing night.

But just as quickly as everything starts, tragedy strikes and threatens to end what we're starting to build.

Can we nurse the spark between us, or will it fizzle out and leave us in the dark?

AUTHOR NOTE

Before the Ashes first appeared in the BABE anthology earlier in 2023. This is the same story, nothing extra has been added but it now has a gorgeous cover of its own.

BEFORE THE ASHES PLAYLIST

Down Under - Men at Work
Wonderwall - Oasis
Every Breath You Take - The Police
With Arms Wide Open - Creed
Over You - Daughtry
Zombie - Bad Wolves
Silence - Blindside
Something In The Way - Nirvana
100 Years - Five For Fighting
All The Right Moves - OneRepublic
Two Is Better Than One - Boys Like Girls feat.
Taylor Swift
She's So High - Cal Bachman
These Day - Powderfinger
The Flame - Cheap Trick

Burning Love - Elvis Presley

Feeling A Moment - Feeder

The Perfect Drug - Nine Ince Nails

Starlight - Muse

Nobody But You - Blake Shelton duet with Gwen
Stefani

The playlist can be found on Spotify.

For my Family

1

TATUM

It's hotter than hell outside today. I'd love nothing more than to laze by the pool here at home with a margarita and my Kindle, but today is the annual gala ball to aid the Lockhart Falls Fire Department. Two things. One, my presence is mandatory. And two, I'm helping Mom with the arrangements. The only excuse for not attending is death, and even then, my ghost would be summoned to appear. This tradition has been occurring since the dawn of the Lockhart Falls Fire Department, or LFFD, *waaaaaaaay* back when the town was founded in the 1800s. This event first started as a family picnic out at Lockhart Falls, and now it's the ball of all balls held at The James Hotel each year. It's become the highlight of the town entertainment calendar, but that isn't hard to achieve since we only have the pickle festival and Christmas fair on the said calendar.

My dad, Shaun Summers, is the current firehouse captain, and it's his responsibility to uphold the tradition. And by him upholding that tradition, it means Mom and I arrange everything. Then he shows up and takes credit for what Mom and I put together. When I was younger, I was expected to help; that's still the case now, even though I'm an LFFD employee for the other three hundred and sixty-four days of the year. I'm twenty-two now, and I've been a full-fledged firefighter for three years. Each year since officially becoming a member of the department, Dad will pull me off shift one day a week, and I become the chief event planner in the weeks leading up to the ball.

The funniest thing about me helping Mom with the ball is I'm the least girly girl you will ever meet. Mom and Dad may have a son and daughter biologically, but in reality, they have two sons. Don't get me wrong, I love a long hot soak in the tub with a glass of wine and a dirty book, but when it comes to dresses and frills and makeup ... thanks but no thanks. Mom, on the other hand, lives for this girly crap. Being designated to help organize this event with her, is my definition of hell, but for the family and tradition, I smile and suck it up. Even if I'd rather run into a burning building or even rescue a cat from a tree—and I fucking hate cats.

"Leaving in ten, Tatum!" Mom yells from downstairs. "We have to meet Madeline to finalize everything as soon as we get there." She's the only one to call me Tatum, everyone else calls me Tate. Well, everyone except my little brother Kain. He calls me Tater-Tot to be annoying. However, I get my revenge and call him Brozart. You see, when he was thirteen, he thought Mozart was a member of the Backstreet Boys, and it's my prerogative as the older sister to never let him live that down.

"Coming!" I yell back.

Tying my blonde hair into a ponytail, I head downstairs to meet Mom so we can head on over to The James Hotel and finalize everything for this evening. Not that there's much to finalize; the event planner there, Madeline "Maddie" Brookes, is *ah-may-zing* at what she does, and Mom and I have been doing this since the beginning of time.

There are two pluses to heading over there today. One, the ballroom and hotel are air-conditioned, so at least I'll be out of this heat. Two, Mom has roped in some of the other firefighters to help today, and that includes Kip Kitson.

Kip is the sexy Australian firefighter who is over here on a twelve-month international fellowship program. This program was started when a group of like-minded captains got together to address the growing challenges of the fire service. This program allows firefighters to learn best practices and internalize the fire service culture in another country. When I say Kip is a sexy Australian, I'm talking if Chris Hemsworth, Hugh Jackman, Heath Ledger—may he rest in peace—and Margot Robbie all had a baby together, it would be Kip Kitson; that's how hot this guy is.

Racing downstairs, I smile when Mom hands me a to-go coffee. "I love you," I declare, smiling at the mug before taking a sip.

"You talking to me or the coffee?"

"Both," I reply with a shrug, causing us both to laugh because we all know I'm a caffeine addict. I drink so much coffee that I wouldn't be surprised if it runs through my veins in place of blood. Taking another sip, I close my eyes and grin. "You make the best coffees Mom; you really should open a coffee shop."

"You'd drink me dry, baby girl." She taps my cheek and walks away from me.

"Yeah, fair point." I shrug. Taking another sip of my lifeblood, I look to Mom, who has her to-go mug in her hand. "Let's do this."

She nods and repeats, "Let's do this." She picks up her handbag and slips the strap over her shoulder, patting the handle to make sure it stays in place. Something we all tease her for doing because hello, OCD much? She grabs her car keys and heads into the living room to say goodbye to Dad and my brother.

Leaning down, she kisses him on the head. "Tatum and I are heading out, we'll be back later. Please, Shaun, I need you and Kain to be showered before we get back, otherwise, we'll be late."

"Yes, dear. Kain and I will be showered and ready," Dad says to Mom, gazing at her with freakin' love hearts in his eyes. Mom and Dad have been together since they were seventeen, and all these years later, they love one another just as fiercely. I want a love like that one day, but for now, I'm gonna have fun and sow my wild oats, as they say. Hopefully I can sow said oats with the sexy Australian import while he's here. I hear that Aussie guys are great down under, and I'm willing to find out if that's true.

"Mom, is it all right if Kip gets ready here too?" My ears perk up at the mention of my Kip, and then I smile when I hear Mom say it's fine, but we're still leaving at six forty-five sharp.

"Later, dudes!" I shout over my shoulder, heading out to the car to wait for Mom.

She arrives just as I click my seat belt into place. She climbs into the driver's seat, and we make our way downtown to The James Hotel. "Thanks for helping out, honey. I know this girly stuff isn't your cup of tea but I appreciate it."

A laugh escapes me but I look to Mom and smile. "You know I'll always help with this, and as much as I'm the definition of a tomboy, I don't mind dressing up every now and again; even if I'd rather stab myself in the face with a rusty fork than wear heels and a ball gown."

"And I appreciate that, I know this is not your idea of fun but seeing you all dressed up is one of the highlights of my year."

"I have to admit, I love seeing everyone dressed up and having fun at this yearly shindig, but I would rather do it in jeans and a hoodie." Mom laughs and shakes her head. "Another highlight? Kain whining and sniveling about having to wear the formal uniform makes it all worth it. May—"

"Nope, you are wearing a dress not the department uniform. Your father agreed, so don't even try to argue with me."

"It sucks being a girl sometimes. Periods. Dresses. Heels and bras, ugh. Girls have such a sucky life."

"It's not that bad," Mom placates. "But all that aside, I love seeing you all dressed up. Your brother looks dashing in his dress uniform. He reminds me of your father at that age. I hope he finds a lady friend one of these days."

"I don't want to think of that, so let's just focus on today."

Mom nods. "I think this year's will be the best one yet. Madeline has been a godsend."

"She sure has and it's Maddie, Mom. I also reckon that great-great, however many greats, Gramps it is, is up there looking down on the event smiling with a pipe between his lips."

"I'm sure he is."

We pull up at the hotel, and I smile when I see the Aussie import already here. His sandy blond hair glows in the morning sunlight. His muscles glisten with sweat and are showcased by the Billabong muscle shirt he's wearing. And I must say, the color of his shirt highlights his amazing tan and physique. Board shorts sit low on his waist, and he completes the outfit with flip-flops, or thongs, as he calls them, on his feet. Hell, even his feet are sexy. How the hell does someone have sexy feet? He's the epitome of an Aussie hunk.

"You've got some drool there on your chin, Sweetie," Mom teases me as she parks the car and turns off the ignition.

"Do not," I snap in reply but I wipe at my chin just to make sure, causing Mom to smirk.

"Yes, dear," she replies in that tone she uses with Dad when she knows she's right and, to reiterate her point, she taps my cheek in that *yeah, yeah* kind of way. "So, you going to try get a look at his fire pole?"

"Moooom, really?" I hiss, ever so thankful she said that before I took a sip, otherwise coffee would be dripping down the front windshield right about now.

"It's just a question," she nonchalantly says with a shrug. "And for what it's worth, I think you and he would make a fine couple."

"Thanks..." I reply but it comes out more like a question.

Sitting in the car, I watch Mom make her way

over to the guys, who are all gathered out front. My eyes immediately find Kip amongst the group, and they drop down to his crotch. Dammit, Mom, now I'm thinking about his fire pole. He looks over at me and smiles and with that one lip lift, I'm gone. Kip Kitson is it for me, game over, end of story. Sorry guys of the world, this one is taken. Smiling back, I climb out of the car, it's time to claim my man ... and set up a ball.

2

KIP

I've been on this international fellowship program for almost two months now. I was over the moon with excitement when I was chosen to participate; it's an amazing opportunity to test and challenge myself. I'm one of the first to be doing a twelve-month exchange, it's usually only six, so I should get the opportunity to learn so much more.

I love living in America. Everything is bigger over here, even the fires. There's no bigger rush than racing into a burning building, well, there is one other rush, seeing Tatum Summers. She is the sexiest woman I have ever seen. She also happens to be the captain's daughter, so she's off-limits, but there's something about the blonde-haired, green-eyed goddess that has me enthralled. She's caught me in her web of hotness, and I'm ready for her to devour me.

"Morning, Mrs. Summers," I greet the captain's wife as she walks over to us. Tatum is still sitting in the car, and I'm almost certain she's checking me out, but the large sunglasses on her face prevent me from confirming if she is or not. She finally climbs out of the car. I'm thankful for my own sunglasses because my eyes pop out of my head as I take her all in. If I was in a cartoon, they'd be extra large and pulsating out of my eye sockets. She's dressed casually in denim cutoff shorts that should be illegal, and a plain black tank with the LFFD logo across it. The fabric hugs her chest, showcasing the most perfect tits I have ever seen in my life.

"There's some drool on your chin," Marcus, one of my colleagues, teases me.

"Fuck off," I whisper-hiss. "It's just sweat since it's hotter than Hades here today." I thought summers in Australia were hot, but here in the middle of California in Lockhart Falls, it's stifling.

Funny story, when I heard I was coming to California, I got my hopes up that I'd be surfing daily and living it up at the beach. Little did this Aussie know, Lockhart Falls is in the middle of nowhere, close to the borders of Nevada and Oregon, and not on the coast, like I presumed *all* of California was. That means the closest ocean is a six-hour drive away, and right now, I'd kill to go to the beach and go surfing to cool down.

That's the one thing I miss from back home—the beaches. Bauckle Beach, where I'm from, is a few hours drive south of Sydney and the hottest place to surf on the South Coast. There's something about diving into the water that resets your body, mind, and soul. Sure, Kain took me to Lockhart Falls a few weekends ago, and it's gorgeous. The crystal-clear waters, white sandy shoreline and magnificent thirty feet tall waterfall are beyond compare. It even has a cave-like grotto behind the falls—that I'm sure many people get down and dirty behind—but give me the beach and waves any day.

The town is named after the falls—real original, I know. I can't really say anything, though. I'm from Bauckle Beach, which was named after Captain Bauckle when he arrived in the late 1700s. It'd be an awesome date location, especially at sunset, because the sun reflecting off the falls is majestic, and seeing your partner in a skimpy bikini is always a thing of beauty. Dammit, now I'm imagining Tatum in a sexy as sin white halter bikini. If only I had the balls to ask her out and turn this dream into a reality.

"You coming?" the girl in question asks me. I totally tuned out while everyone was discussing the plans, and now I have no clue what's going on. I bet I've been given a shitty task to complete but giving me some alone time with her right now is totally worth any crap job.

"Yeah, sure," I respond, hoping my tone doesn't give away how clueless I am right now.

"Is the California heat getting to you, kangaroo boy?"

"Kangaroo boy, really?"

"Vegemite kid?" she offers as an alternative with a shrug. I can't help but laugh. Tatum has been the only person so far to enjoy Vegemite, which reminds me, I should make her some of my famous Vegemite and cheese scrolls. She loved the chicken parmigiana I made the other week when Shaun and Ginny invited me over.

"Yeah, let's just stick with Kip."

"Okay, Kip." The way she says my name has my dick perking up. "Are you coming?" Her choice of words has me thinking *very soon*. I've never felt a pull like this to a woman before, and never has asking such an innocent question, like "are you coming?" sparked such a visceral reaction from my body. Ever. Tatum Summers might very well be the death of me, and I'm good with that. Death by Tatum would be an amazing way to die.

Standing here, I watch her walk into the hotel, and I shake my head. It's going to be a hot one today, and I'm not referring to the weather.

3

TATUM

"Mom, can we go already? Everything looks great," I whine for the millionth time.

"Don't rush me, Tatum," she snaps. "This has—"

"To be perfect," I interrupt her because we've had the same conversation every day of my life. "And it is mom." Ginny Summers is a perfectionist, so much so, that in the dictionary, her picture would be next to the definition of the word, but you know what? I wouldn't change a thing. My mom is perfect in every way a mom should be. Sure, it's annoying at times, like now, but when Mom puts her mind to something, she sees it through. It's always perfect, beyond perfect, because she goes above and beyond what's expected and she cares. It's her biggest trait, and her biggest flaw.

"You really think so?"

"I know so," I confirm with a nod.

"And I agree," Maddie says, joining us. "I think this is the best event I have ever had the privilege of helping set up."

"We couldn't have done it without you, Madeline," Mom says, smiling brightly at Maddie, who I'm sure will berate Mom for calling her Madeline in three … two … one.

"I'm sure you would have, Ginny. You two ladies make a great team." Hmmmpf, she didn't berate Mom. "And please, call me Maddie." *There it is.* I grin to myself at calling it.

"Thank you, Maddie," Mom replies, finally calling her Maddie. "Will you and Penn be joining us tonight?"

"Unfortunately, no, we're heading away for the weekend. It's our first wedding anniversary, and I have a surprise for him." She rubs her flat belly, and I realize she's pregnant.

"I knew you were!" Mom squeals. "You have that baby glow about you. Congratulations to you both."

"Thank you, it was a surprise but a welcome one."

"Those kinds of surprises are the best. My Tatum was a surprise like that."

Her phone begins to ring, and I'm guessing it's her husband because her face lights up. "I need to get this but if you need anything tonight, I'm just a phone call away."

Before either of us can say that we'll be fine, she answers the phone and walks away. Mom starts to look around, and I know if I don't get her out of here now, we'll be here for another hour. I grab our bags, link my arm with hers, and lead her toward the exit. Shocking the crap out of me, she willingly comes with me.

We climb into the car and head home to get ready for the evening. Opening the front door, Mom stops suddenly, causing me to bump into her. When I look over her shoulder and see Dad, I know why she stopped. He's standing in the hallway, decked out in his dress uniform, and in his arms is a huge bouquet of sunflowers for Mom. "Did I do good, Ginny?"

Mom nods and even though I'm behind her, I bet she has tears in her eyes. That thought is confirmed when she lifts her hand and wipes at her eye. Dad starts walking toward her. "For you my love," he says, handing Mom the flowers and placing a kiss on her cheek. He looks at me and winks before turning his gaze back to Mom.

"I'll, ummm, go get ready," I tell them both; they nod but neither say anything. They just continue to eye-fuck one another—gag. Not wanting to bear witness to this anymore, I quickly step around them and head toward the stairs. I take them two at a time, and when I'm halfway up, I look back and my heart soars when I see Mom and Dad together. He's cupping her cheek, and they are quietly talking to one another, oblivious to everything around them. They are so in love and have set the bar extremely high for what I want when I find my one true love. One day, I hope to have a love like them.

Entering my room, I throw my bag on my bed and walk into the adjoining bathroom that I share with my brother. Closing the door to Kain's room, I reach into the shower, turn the water on, and close the door, letting it fill with steam while I strip off.

Once naked, I jump into the shower and let out a moan when the hot, steamy water cascades down my body. Dropping my head back, I close my eyes and stand under the stream. Knowing I don't have long to get ready, I quickly shave my legs, wash my body, and then my hair.

Stepping out, I grab a towel for my hair and flip my head upside down. I give the strands a quick dry, and then I wrap the towel around my head like a turban. When I stand up straight, I come face-to-face with Kip. He's standing in the doorway to Kain's room, dressed only in a towel. A towel that's sitting low on his hips, showcasing that illusive V that cause women to go gaga over—hello, I'm said woman—and I have an unobstructed view of his rippled abs. His skin is golden brown from the hot Australian sun, and I want to lick him from head to toe.

His gaze peruses my body, much like what I'm doing to his.

The air in the room heats, and it's not from the leftover steam from my shower. Sadly, the moment—if you can call it a moment—is broken when I hear Kain yell, "Tate, fuck, you're naked. Put some fucking clothes on ... and *you*." He looks to Kip and slaps him upside the head. "Stop eye-fucking my sister." That snaps me into action, and I quickly grab my towel and wrap it around my body.

Now that I'm covered, I turn around and head into my room, closing the door behind me. Leaning back against it, I shake my head and grin. I cannot believe he just saw me naked. Now I think it's only fair that he gives me a glimpse at what's below his towel.

TATUM IS GORGEOUS WITH CLOTHES ON, BUT naked and wet after stepping out of the shower, fuck me sideways, she's a walking wet dream. If Kain didn't walk in when he did, who knows what he would have walked in on a few moments later.

After seeing her like that, I need to date her now.

"Dude, that was my sister you were just eye-fucking," Kain growls, punching me in the shoulder after slamming the door to their joined bathroom shut. "Why did I invite you to get ready here?" He shakes his head and drops down onto the end of his bed.

"Dude, have you seen your sister? She's fucking hot," I reply with a shrug.

"That's. My. Sister." He emphasizes each word, glaring at me.

"Your point?" I throw back at him with a cheeky grin, taunting him right now is too easy.

"Seriously, dude, she's my—"

"Sister, I get it but, I ... well, I've kinda had a crush on her since I arrived, and after seeing her in there just now ..." I nod toward the closed bathroom door. "I *reeeaaaally* want to get to know her now." That comment earns me another punch. "Ouch, you asshole."

"Stop mentioning my naked sister."

"I didn't say she was naked."

"You implied it, same thing."

"Whatever, but seriously, I like her. I ... I want to get to know her."

"So go for it," he tells me, shocking the shit out of me. I was expecting more of a brotherly, protective *touch her you die* response, not a *go for it* one.

"Really?"

"Yeah. You're a good guy from what I've seen so far, plus, you're Australian *and* a firefighter, can't get any cooler than that."

"Really? You didn't think I was so awesome when I gave you a taste of Vegemite."

"That shit's nasty, and you liking that crap is

your only downfall. Grossmite aside, I actually think you and her would be perfect together, and I must say, you're way better than the douchehole assholes she usually goes for."

"You really think that?" I question him again. I'm still waiting for him to turn around and tell me he's joking and that I need to back the fuck off when it comes to his sister. I know if I had a sister I'd be all protective of her but him giving me the green light has thrown me for a loop.

"Yeah, I do. Plus, she's old enough to make her own decisions. Just know, you hurt her and you will be heading back down under—six feet down under. Capiche?"

"Capiche, really? Are you suddenly in the mob?"

"When it comes to my sister, I will do whatever it takes to keep her safe and happy."

"Okay, thanks, man, but do you think she likes me?" I realize that last question makes me sound like a pussy, but I need to know.

"There's only one way to find out." He picks up his shoes and leaves the bedroom. Dropping my towel, I finish getting dressed for tonight, and as I button up my shirt, I start to wonder if Tatum is on the same page as her brother.

Walking downstairs, I hear chatter in the living room, and when I step in, I pause at the entrance, my eyes immediately finding Tatum. I stand here and stare over at her, she's wearing a halter-style, dark blue, almost black, ball gown that hugs her curves and is sexy as hell. The back is open, and it obviously ties around the neck as down the center of her back is a silk tie. If I thought she was sexy from the back, I'm left speechless and the breath is knocked out of me when she turns around. I was expecting—*hoping* —to get a view of her gorgeous tits. However, the material of her dress goes all the way up to her neck, exposing her shoulders, and that's somehow sexier than if her chest and tits were on display. The top cinches in at her waist and flows down to the carpet. I don't know shit about ball gowns but this is the sexiest one I have ever seen.

"Kip," Mrs. Summers says when she notices me. "Don't you look dashing." At her compliment, a smile breaks free. It's not often I get to wear my dress uniform, and I'm thankful for that because I'm a boardies and T-shirt kind of guy. I must admit though, it's nice to dress up occasionally ... especially if it means I get to see Tate like this.

"Thank you, Mrs. Summers."

"What have I told you, call me Ginny."

"Thank you, Ginny," I reply with a smile before looking to Tatum. "You look beautiful, Tate."

"Thanks," she shyly replies, brushing her golden blonde locks over her shoulders, highlighting them. I've never found shoulders to be sexy before but right now, I'm a shoulders man.

"Everyone ready?" Captain Summers asks as he joins us.

"Just waiting on Kain," Ginny replies.

"I'm here," he breathlessly says, joining us.

"Fix your tie, Son," Captain Summers growls at Kain. Kain's uniform isn't the final formal one since he's only a cadet.

"It's fine, Dad," he throws back, earning himself a glare from his dad.

"Mine is fine, yours is crappy, now fix it. We're not leaving this house with you dressed like that."

"Geesh, Dad, chill," Kain says with a headshake and an eyeroll.

"Let me," Ginny offers to keep the peace. One thing I've noticed since being here is Kain and his dad butt heads all the time, especially when it comes to work. Ginny walks over to Kain and fixes his tie, not that there was much to fix. Shaun Summers is a man to be reckoned with, and he's someone I highly respect so I keep my mouth shut and watch as Ginny fusses over her son.

"Perfect, now, let's go." The Captain links arms with Ginny, and the five of us head outside to the Summers's SUV.

"After you," I offer to Tatum since she'll be sitting in the middle. She smiles and climbs in, and I take the opportunity to check out her ass. Probably a bad move because my dick twitches, and if it gets any harder, I'm going to have a zipper imprint on it. Thinking of fat naked ladies with saggy tits, my dick softens, and I climb in behind her.

We arrive at The James Hotel and I climb out. Turning around, I offer Tatum my hand, and when she places hers in mine, I swear I feel a jolt of electricity zap between us. Going by the wide-eyed expression on her face, she felt it too. I'm still holding her hand and staring at her when a commotion by the door causes both of us to avert our gaze from one another and drop hands. We see Kain's best friend, Burton Hayes, and his girlfriend, Trina *I'm a Drama Queen Michels* having a fight, again. Why he sticks with her, I will never know. I'm all for dating a hot chick but I don't do drama. They go their separate ways with her storming to the car and Burton heading inside, alone, no doubt heading to the bar to drown his sorrows.

Now that the drama is over, I look back to Tatum. She smiles at me, and then she shocks me when she laces our fingers together and leads us inside. Hand in hand, we follow the rest of the Summers family. Maybe Kain was right and Tatum feels what I feel too. So I tell myself that tonight ... tonight I'm going to make Tatum Summers mine.

5

TATUM

Kip's hand fits in mine as if we were cast in the same mold. Hand in hand, we walk into the ballroom and head toward our table. I notice all eyes are on us. I don't know why everyone is staring, it's not like I haven't turned up to this ball with a date before. Not that Kip is officially my date, maybe they're all staring because there's just a hot Aussie firefighter escorting me to my table.

"Everyone's staring at us," he whispers to me, his breath skates over my skin causing goosebumps to appear.

"That's 'cause you're hot," I inform him.

"No, I think it's because you're the belle of the ball, but thanks for the compliment."

"If the hotness fits, I'll shout it out for the world to know."

"Well, in that case, it should be me shouting to the world because you, Tatum Summers, are fucking ravishing tonight. I'm not sure what's hotter, you dressed up like this or you naked and dripping wet."

"Maybe we need to do a side-by-side comparison sometime," I reply, raising my eyebrows suggestively at him. Where is this sex bomb version of me coming from? I don't flirt with guys like this; I'm not *that* girl.

"Fuck, Tate, you can't say shit like that to me now. I'm going to be sporting a woodie all night now, and my boss, who also happens to be your dad, is sitting across from me."

Shrugging at him, I go to pull my chair out but, ever the gentleman, he pulls it out for me. "Why thank you."

"Anything for a pretty lady."

"I might just have to prove too you later how much of a lady I'm not," I playfully reply, batting my eyelashes up at him.

He shakes his head and slides into the seat next to me, resting his arm across the back of my chair. "You are going to be the death of me, woman."

"Please don't die, the world needs a hot Aussie firefighter in it."

"So, you think I'm hot?"

"We've already established that, but I have to say, I really want to see what you're packing under that towel you were wearing."

"Check, please," he sings out, raising his hand as if to signal the waiter. That causes me to laugh but my laugh sticks when he begins to run his fingertip across my exposed back, and now, I'm thinking he's going to be the death of me.

Kip and I are getting along so well. It's fun and playful. Something I haven't felt with a guy for a very long time. With training at the academy and then working, I haven't really had time to date, plus most guys here know of our family and my dad, and no one wants to fuck the captain's daughter. Well, maybe Kip does but he's only here as part of the IFP program. It's just fun and games for him, and I think I'd be okay with just some fun.

"You're a goofball," I tell him.

"A sexy goofball, right?"

"Maybe," I coyly reply as I take a sip of the champagne that magically appeared before me.

"I'll take that as a yes." He taps his glass of magically appearing bubbly against mine and takes a sip. I watch as he swallows and the bob of his Adam's apple does things to me that shouldn't be happening when it comes to a freakin Adam's apple. "And for the record, you, Tatum Summers, are the sexiest firefighter I have ever seen." He leans in closer, and his breath fans across my neck. "One day, I'm going to make you my wife, Tatum Summers, and we are going to have gorgeous firefighter babies and live happily ever after," he whispers. His admission causes me to choke on my drink. I rapidly blink at him as I process his words. "Now, if you'll excuse me, I'm heading to the bar, I need a Fireball whiskey shot and a beer. Bubbly isn't my jam."

"That sounds delish, mind if I join you?"

"Not at all, let's go get our drink on."

The evening is drawing to a close, and I have to say, tonight's ball has been the best one yet—and it's not just because of the man I'm currently slow dancing with. The food is phenomenal, the band is awesome, and the man whose arms I'm currently in has been an amazing date, even if technically this wasn't a date. Kip is funny, considerate, sexy as hell, and man, can he dance.

"This night has been amazing," he murmurs.

"I was just thinking the same thing. Do you ..." But I don't finish because suddenly I'm nervous.

"Do I what?"

"Umm, want to get out of here? Maybe head back to your place?"

He nods at me. "I think I'd like that, but before we do that, I just need to do one thing."

"Okay, sure. I'll grab my things and wait for you."

He shakes his head side to side. "No, what I need to do is right here, I need to kiss you."

My breath hitches in my throat. I swallow hard, and my tongue darts out and wets my lip. "So kiss me," I murmur.

We stare at one another intently, and then, as if a force has us trapped in its vortex, our faces drift closer together. He tilts his head to the left, I tilt mine to the right, and our lips touch. Like when I took his hand earlier, sparks fly. Angels sing. Fireworks explode. He pushes his tongue into my mouth, and I moan at the intrusion. Our tongues slip and slide languidly back and forth. Draping my arms over his shoulders, I pull him into me, deepening the connection between us. He wraps his arms around my waist, and I can feel his erection pressing into my stomach. I like what I feel.

"Let's get out of here," I pant against his lips

when I break away from the best kiss in the history of kisses.

"Let's," he breathlessly whispers back.

Lacing our fingers together, we make our way back to the table, and as we approach, I see Mom and Dad. Both are grinning like Ronald freaking McDonald. "What?" I nonchalantly ask as I reach over for my clutch.

"Your mother owes me a golf weekend away," Dad tells me, and somehow his grin widens farther.

"Huh?" I ask, my face scrunched in confusion.

"Your father and I had a bet on how long it would be before you two kissed. I said Thanksgiving, he said it would happen tonight," Mom explains, while dad just sits there grinning over his win.

"You bet on how long it would be before Kip and I kissed?" They both nod. "Seriously?" They both nod again. "What? Why would you do that?"

"Your father and I have been making bets like this our whole relationship, it's not often he gets a win in, hence, why I agreed to his golf weekend away because I was sure I'd win."

"What would you have gotten if we waited 'til Thanksgiving?"

"A diamond bracelet from Tiffany's."

"Seriously? What else have you bet on?"

"What your mother and I bet on stays between your mother and me. It's the first rule of Bet Club."

Shaking my head, I chuckle at Dad. "That was corny, Dad."

"Hey, I won a weekend of golfing, I'll be as corny as I like." He then looks to Kip. "You hurt her and I'll make you disappear. I know how to make a death by fire look accidental."

"Duly noted, sir, but I don't plan on hurting her."

"Good, good. You two have a great night, use protect—"

"Daaaaad," I protest.

He smirks. "And I expect to see you both for Sunday dinner."

With that uncomfortable warning and the demand for dinner, I kiss my parents goodbye before Kip and I head outside to wait for our Uber since we both arrived with my parents.

He wraps his arms around me from behind, nuzzles my neck, and whispers, "I can't wait to get you home, Tatum. I sure hope you aren't planning on getting any sleep tonight."

6

___

KIP

SITTING IN THE BACK OF THE UBER, I KEEP glancing over at Tate. Expecting to see her vanish before my eyes because surely this is a dream, and any moment now I'll be alone in the back of this car.

"You keep staring at me," Tatum utters, breaking the silence. "Do I have something on my face?"

"No, you look beautiful. I just keep thinking that this is a dream."

"Does this feel like a dream to you?" She reaches over and runs her hand up my thigh and cups my junk in her palm, gently squeezing.

"No dream has felt like that before."

"I assure you, Kip, this is one-million-percent real."

"Maybe you should kiss me so I can really make sure."

"For the sake of putting your mind at ease, I guess I can kiss you again." She unclips her seat belt, shimmies across the seat, and climbs sideways onto my lap. She grips my cheeks and lowers her lips to mine. Closing my eyes, I slide my hand up her back and into her hair. Cupping the nape of her neck, I hold her against me and kiss her back. While the kiss on the dance floor was slow, this one is hurried and frenzied. Our tongues fight for dominance. Our teeth clash. Our lips push together with force. "Is that real enough for you?"

"Maybe you should let me see what's hiding under this sexy as sin dress, you know, for peace of mind."

"I'm sure that can be arranged. Personally, I'm not one for fucking in public, so you will have to patiently wait 'til we're back at your place. I won't be opposed to kissing you again, though."

We stare at one another, but the moment is broken when the driver declares, "Get out of my car and then you kids can start your lesson or whatever the fuck in private. We're here." He chuckles to himself, and I realize we're back at my apartment complex.

"Thanks, man," I tell him.

Tate slides off my lap, and I get out, offering her my hand, she takes it and climbs out behind me. Just as I close the door, I hear the driver mumble, "Ohhh to be young and in love again." Slamming the door closed, I tap the roof, and he pulls away from the curb.

Taking Tate's hand, we walk toward the entrance and head inside for a night that I hope is the start of something beautiful.

7

TATUM

Walking into the building with Kip, my heart is racing. I've been with guys before, but never have I felt a connection like I do with Kip. It's almost as if our souls intertwined the moment we kissed. Angels sang and the heavens above cheered about our union because I've found my soul mate. Now that I have him, I'm never letting him go. It's crazy to feel like this since we only kissed for the first time less than an hour ago, but it feels like we're meant to be. I can feel it deep inside. I can't explain why I feel like this, and I'm not going to analyze it, I'm just going to live in the moment and give my everything to this.

While I'm internalizing the events of tonight up until this moment, we enter the elevator and make it up to Kip's apartment. Our hands are still clasped, each of us holding on for dear life, scared that if we let go, we'll part ways, never to see one another again.

"After you," he drawls in that sexy Aussie accent of his. Stepping inside, he flicks the lights on, and I'm pleasantly surprised when I glance around his open plan apartment. I was expecting a bright place since Kip is so outgoing and always the life of the room but instead, it's all grays, blacks, and whites. Muted and not Kip-like but at the same time, it fits him.

"You are so fucking gorgeous, Tatum," he whispers from behind me. Looking back at him over my shoulder, I smile. "You in that dress has had me at half-mast most of the evening."

"You look pretty spiffy yourself, Kip."

"Thanks, but do you want to know what I really think about your dress?" Nodding, I swallow deeply, waiting for his reply. He steps closer to me and runs his fingertip up my exposed spine. Grabbing my loose locks, he moves my hair over my shoulder, leans in, and murmurs, "It would look much better on the floor."

Nodding again and feeling brave, I keep my eyes locked on his, silently reach behind my neck, and tug on the bow. When the knot comes free, I pull it around to the front, and the dress slides down my body and flutters to the hardwood floor below, leaving me only in a black, skimpy G-string and my heels. "Better?" I huskily murmur.

He steps away from me, and I immediately miss the feel of him pressed against my back. "I think I might need a look from the front."

Spinning around, I face him. He's still fully dressed, and I'm practically naked, but never have I felt sexier than I do in this moment. "Fuck me, Tate—"

"That's the plan," I inform him with a teasing tone. "But we seem to have a problem."

"I don't see a problem at all," he tells me matter-of-factly. "All I see is the sexiest woman I have ever seen in my life, naked in my apartment."

"And I see the sexiest man I have ever seen in my life but, you sir, are overdressed."

"Well, we better fix that then."

"Let me," I offer.

Reaching up, I pull on his tie, and when it's loose enough, I lift it over his head and drop it to join my dress. Then one by one, I pop open the buttons on his shirt, revealing his tanned, toned, muscular chest. Tugging it out of his pants, I slide the material off his shoulders, and it flutters to the floor below, pillowing at our feet. I take a few moments to ogle him, and then I start work on his pants. With nimble fingers I undo his belt, pop the button, and lower his fly. As I push his pants down his legs, I drop to my knees and come face-to-face with his bulging cock confined in his briefs. Licking my lips, I free his dick, and my eyes widen when I see it in the flesh for the first time. It's girthy. It's long, and I cannot wait to wrap my lips around it.

Licking my lips, I lean forward and place a kiss on the glistening tip, earning myself a hiss from above. That hiss turns into a guttural moan when I open wide and suck his shaft into my mouth. My lips wrap around him, and I slide his cock in and out of my wet mouth. "Fuck, Tate," he breathlessly whispers when I relax my throat and take him all the way in. Kip threads his fingers into my hair and gently guides my head back and forth. Lifting my hand, I cup his balls and fondle them. With my other hand, I press on that spot at the base of his shaft and between his anus, causing him to shudder. With that, the first spurt of hot, salty cum shoots into my mouth. He grunts through his release, and I suck and swallow every drop.

Dropping back on my heels, I stare up at a blissfully sated Kip. He opens his eyes and gazes down at me. "That was an unexpected yet fucking amazing surprise, but now it's my turn to bring you pleasure." Before I have time to blink, Kip bends down, kicks off his briefs, lifts me up, throws me over his shoulder, slaps me on the ass, and marches into his bedroom.

He throws me down onto the bed. A squeal slips out as I bounce on the mattress. Kip grips my ankles and pulls me toward him at the end of the bed. He lifts my left leg, resting my foot on his shoulder, then kisses my ankle and trails his lips up my calf. He moves along the inside of my thigh and up to the apex of my groin. Running his nose along my panty-covered vagina, he inhales. "You smell like heaven," he pants. His nose nudges my clit, and he licks along my folds. I moan at the sensation, and even though there's a thin strip of material creating a barrier between his tongue and my flesh, I can feel everything as if he's licking me skin on skin. My hips arch up, wanting more. He presses on my stomach, pushing me down as he continues to lick me through my panties.

"Please," I moan, cupping my breasts and tugging on my nipples.

He lifts his head and watches me play with my boobs. "Fuck, that's hot."

"You know what would be hotter?"

"What?"

"Your penis in my vagina." Raising my eyebrows at him, I then flick my gaze from his dick to my vagina.

"I think that can be arranged," he croons as he reaches over and grabs a condom from somewhere. Tearing open the foil packet, he slides it on and then reaches down and grabs the edge of my panties. I go to lift up so he can pull them down my legs, but he shocks me and tears them from my body. He literally rips my panties from me, the material disintegrating in his fingers, leaving me naked before him. He discards the torn material over his shoulder, spreads my legs wide, and teases my entrance with the tip of his dick.

"Kip," I warn. He chuckles but finally gives me what I want, and with the flick of his hips, he presses his head between my folds and finally enters me. My pussy stretches around him. I've never been so full before; it's slightly painful but he pulls out and slams back in. With each thrust, that pain is replaced by the most delightful feeling in the world.

With his eyes locked on mine, he slides in and out of me, each thrust bringing me to a new height of pleasure. Sex has never felt this fantabulous before, and I never want it to end. My body is thrumming from head to toe. Each nerve ending is alight, zinging in the most pleasurable way. That tingling feeling begins to develop low in my belly, and then, out of nowhere, the most intense climax ever explodes. My body stiffens, and wave after wave of euphoria crashes through my body. My pussy walls clench around Kip, and he comes with a growl that I'm sure can be heard in Australia. He empties his seed into the condom, his body shuddering above me as he rides out his climax.

Pulling out, he collapses onto the bed next to me. Both of us lie here, blissfully panting. Neither of us utters a word, but no words are needed. The moment is perfect in every way. After one time, I'm addicted to this man, and I never want to let him go.

8

KIP

WAKING UP WITH A NAKED TATE NEXT TO ME is the best feeling in the world. Last night was everything and more. Last night, it felt like my soul found its mate, and I'm finally whole. After jumping from foster family to foster family growing up, it's an awesome feeling to finally feel complete. There was always a part of me that was empty, that was missing, but being with Tate these past twelve hours filled that gap. I really hope this is the start of something beautiful between us and not just one hot and heavy night.

"Morning," she huskily mumbles from next to me. Her voice is sleep riddled but it vibrates over me, causing me to smile and my dick to stir.

Turning my head, I take her in, and she looks

just as sexy with bed hair, sleep in her eyes, and smeared makeup. "Morning, beautiful," I whisper, brushing a tendril of hair behind her ear and cupping her cheek in my palm. Leaning over for a morning kiss, I press my lips to hers and close my eyes. Her tongue pushes into my mouth and what was meant to be a quick nonsexual morning peck on the lips turns into more.

So.

Much.

More.

Tate shimmies closer to me, and when I feel her nipples press into my chest, it's game on. Wrapping my arms around her, I pull her closer to me. My morning wood presses into her stomach. She moans into my mouth, and before I know what's happening, she pushes me to my back and straddles me. My dick just so happens to slide into her warm, wet, inviting pussy, wishing it a good morning. With her eyes locked on mine, she begins to ride me.

Her eyes close. Her head drops back, and she gives herself over to the pleasure. She lifts her hands and cups her boobs. Watching her pleasure herself is mesmerizing but I need to touch her. Reaching up, I push her hands out of the way and cup her tits in my palms. I tenderly massage her plump mounds before I gently pinch her nipples.

"Suck them," she purrs, and who am I to deny her?

Lifting myself up, I slide one hand around her back, anchoring her to me, and with the other, I guide her breast to my mouth and suck.

"Yesssssss," she hisses through clenched teeth. Gently I bite down, marking her breast, earning myself another sexy as fuck moan.

"I'm close," she pants.

"Look at me," I demand. She lifts her head and opens her eyes. With our gazes locked on one another, we push ourselves over the edge, and in unison, we growl each other's names as we tumble into the abyss and through our release.

She rests her forehead against mine, and we stare at one another. Our hurried breaths mingle together as we come back to Earth. "Now that's a morning kiss," she pants.

"I'll expect wake-up sex like that anytime you're in my bed, please," I playfully demand.

She nods and grins. "I think I can handle that." She presses her lips to mine and this time, we just kiss. Breaking the kiss, she pulls back. "I guess, umm, I, ahh, better get going then."

"Yep," I dejectedly reply, but really, I don't want her to leave.

"Oooooorrrrrr," she offers. "We could order in breakfast and maybe snuggle a little longer?"

"I think I like that option best, but it all depends on one thing ..."

"And what might that one thing be?"

"We have naked Sunday, and after breakfast, I get to lick maple syrup off your body."

She taps her chin, purses her lips, and thinks. "You have yourself a deal, Kip Kitson, but before we order breakfast, you should fuck me in the shower. You know, to be hygienically clean for breakfast and your maple-covered Tate dessert."

"You drive a hard bargain, Ms. Summers, but I think I can abide by your rules."

"From where I'm sitting, Mr. Kitson, it's you who's hard." She grips my once again hard cock, causing me to hiss." She jumps off the bed and offers me her hand. "Now, lead the way to my shower fuck."

9

TATUM

THIS MORNING AND LAST NIGHT HAVE BEEN amazing with Kip. I had high expectations. I can firmly say each and every one of them was smashed to smithereens ... much like my vagina. I don't think I've ever had that much sex in one night, let alone out-of-this-world, amazing sex. I was worried it was only going to be a one-time deal with Kip, but I was wrong, so very wrong. We christened every surface in his apartment, and while we didn't broach the subject per se, I think we might be dating now. In amongst the best fucking sex of my life marathon, Kip and I chatted and chatted and chatted. He told me all about his childhood. He had a rough start in life but due to his determination, he's jumped over some tough hurdles and has grown into an amazing guy, who I learned doesn't have a middle name.

Kip Kitson is someone I could quite easily see myself falling in love with. He's someone I can see myself settling down with, too, but there's one obstacle in our way. One *huuuuuuuuuge* ten-thousand-mile obstacle. He lives in Australia, and I live in Lockhart Falls, California. Maybe I'm getting ahead of myself and it's a moot point, but the thought of never seeing Kip again kills me.

"What are you thinking so hard about?" Kip asks as I finish drying off after our sexy, orgasm-filled shower. Wrapping the towel around my body, I see Kip has done the same. However, I still get to ogle his chest and abs, making me want to lick each and every crevice on his stomach before licking down his V and taking his cock into my mouth ... again. One night with this guy and I've turned into a sex addict—and I will happily admit to that. *Hi, my name is Tatum Prudence Summers and I'm addicted to sex with Kip "no middle name" Kitson.*

"Nothing in particular," I lie. I can't tell him what I'm really thinking because it will scare him off. It's crazy to be thinking about this stuff after one night but I literally can't stop thinking about it, or the amazing sex—see? Addict. I can't tell him that I want to suck and lick him again because that will make me sound like a sex-crazed whore, and I don't want to scare the guy off.

"I call bullshit." He reaches out and pulls me into him. Sliding his hands around my back, he stares intently at me. "Now, tell me what you're thinking— without lying this time."

"You're going to think I'm a crazy chick with possible stalker tendencies."

"You'd be wrong, I'd be thinking you're a sexy crazy chick with stalker tendencies who I think is fabulous in every way, and if I was ever to have a stalker, I'd want one as hot as you."

"Now who's crazy?" I tease him back.

"Crazy for you," he says, nuzzling my nose with his, but hearing those words makes my heart skip a beat, and it gives me the confidence to tell him what I was thinking just now. "So, now that we know we're both crazy, do you wanna tell me what you were thinking?"

Nodding my head, I decide to just go for it. What's the worst that'll happen? He'll kick me out and never look at me again? I can deal with that. Taking a deep breath, I tell him exactly what I was thinking. "Last night, I felt something with you, Kip. Something I've never felt before, and the thought of you going home sucks donkey dick. I really don't want you to go back to Australia."

"I'm not leaving for ten months."

"I know that but ..." I drift off, not wanting to voice my fear because it will just reaffirm that this is temporary.

"But what? You can be honest with me."

"I know I can. When I'm around you, I'm the me'est me I can be, and I don't want you to leave because I want more. I want it all with you, Kip."

When I finish my ramblings, he just stares at me. He doesn't utter a word. My fear of him thinking I'm crazy bubbles to the surface, but then he reaches up and cups my cheek in his palm. "Tatum Prudence Summers, I feel the same way you do. It's crazy to feel this after just one fucking amazing, out-of-this-world night and morning, but I feel like you're the missing piece of my soul. Now that I've found you, I don't want to let you go. I'm dreading the thought of leaving you in ten months' time, but do you know what I think?"

"What?"

"I think if we're meant to be, we will be." He runs this thumb along my jaw, and it relaxes me. One little thumb movement eases all my worries. "So, I say, for the next ten months, we live life to the fullest.

We do everything together, and when my time here is up, we'll know what's meant to happen next, but I'm willing to bet my left nut that you and I will be together and planning the next adventure of Kipum."

"Kipum, really?"

"Yep, it's our celebrity name, and once you have one of those, you've made it."

"You really think that? You don't think the whole *leaving to go back down under* part of the equation will hinder us being a Kipum?"

"It only will if we let it. So, how about I make us some Vegemite toast, and then I can spend the rest of the day buried balls deep inside of you?"

"I thought there was going to be maple syrup too?"

"I'm sure that can be arranged but before we do any of that, I need to kiss you."

"Then kiss me."

He reaches up and cups both my cheeks in his palms and presses his lips to mine. It's soft. It's sensual. It's the perfect kiss, but there's one problem. I'm hornier than I was before, and knowing that there's only a thin cotton towel separating our bodies, it's giving me all sorts of wicked dirty ideas that once again involve my tongue on his abs and ending with my lips wrapped around his dick. Kip seems to have the same idea because my towel is suddenly ripped away, leaving me naked.

"Oops," he playfully says before dropping to his knees and lifting my leg over his shoulder. He leans forward and licks me from taint to clit. My body comes alive under his touch and I need more. As if he's in my head, he gives me more. He suckles on my clit and shoves a finger inside of me. Drawing it out, he thrusts it in again and again. Unabashedly, I ride his hand and face. Gripping his golden locks, I press myself into him farther.

I've become the wanton whore I was worried about, but right now, I don't care. I'm going to whore away and give myself over to the pleasure building within. I'm on the brink of my climax when I feel a pressure against my anus. My eyes widen, and I open my mouth to protest but he pushes his finger into my ass and I explode. Dots mar my vision, and I scream out like a banshee. I come harder than I have ever come before. My body quivers. My legs turn to jelly, and I'm ready to collapse. If it wasn't for Kip's grip on me, I'd be a completely sated heap on the bathroom floor.

Kip removes his face from between my thighs, flops onto his ass, and pulls me down into his lap.

Straddling him, I rapidly blink and breathe heavily. "Holy shit, I nearly passed out from that orgasm."

"You're welcome," he playfully replies. "Now, how about breakfast?"

"What about you?" I ask, dropping my gaze to his rock-hard dick between us.

"I won't say no to a BJ, but I thought you wanted food?"

"I do want food but I want that"—and to reiterate the 'that' I want, I grip his dick in my hand and squeeze—"more. Let me blow you, and then we can eat."

"You had me at blow."

He leans back on his hands and waggles his eyebrows suggestively at me. Waggling mine back at him, I continue to stroke him through the towel. "Fuuuuuck," he groans, dropping his head back. Seeing him like that turns me on again but it's not about me right now. Right now, it's all about him. Shuffling back, I push the towel aside and stroke him, skin on skin. He hisses and seeing the look of euphoria on his face encourages me to continue.

Lowering my head down, I take his cock into my mouth and suck on the tip, swirling my tongue around, I lick his slit. "Fuuuuuck, Tate, your mouth is divine."

"Hmmmhmpf," I mumble around his shaft.

Sliding my lips down his shaft, I bob my head back and forth, gently raking my teeth along his skin in an upward motion. Kip grips my head and guides me up and down, in sync with his hips thrusting upward. Pushing down farther and farther with each stroke, the tip hits the back of my throat, and I gag a little, but that seems to spur him on. As if he can sense what I can take, he never pushes too far. Again that, *this is perfect and right* feeling washes over me, and I smile around his dick.

"I'm close," he pants.

Reaching up, I cup his balls and press on that spot between the base of his shaft and his ass, and it sends him over the edge. His body stiffens and the first spurt of salty cum hits my tongue. Swallowing each and every last drop, I pull off his dick and sit up.

"You have a fucking magical mouth."

"Why thank you," I tell him, and if I was standing up, I'd curtsy and possibly suck his dick again—once again reaffirming myself as an addicted sex-crazed whore.

We stare at one another silently, but the moment is broken when my cell starts to ring. "I better get that."

"Yep." He nods but neither of us makes a move,

and the phone stops ringing. It immediately starts to ring again, as does Kip's. He scrunches his face once the ringtone is more prominent. He's one of those weirdos who allocates ringtones to different people. "That's the firehouse," he says, and if mine is also ringing, it must be something bad.

Lifting off of him, we exit the bathroom and each answer our phones.

"Hey, Daddy," I say in greeting.

"Hey, Munchkin, sorry to bother you on your day off but we need all-hands-on-deck. A warehouse in the industrial area is ablaze, and it's threatening the chemical factory next door."

"I'll be there in five," I tell him.

"Bring Kip with you," he says and hangs up before I can say goodbye.

Turning to Kip, I see he already has a pair of sweats on and another pair in his hands. "Thought you might want to wear these so you don't have to wear last night's dress ... even if last night's dress is much sexier than a pair of my sweats."

"Thanks." I take the sweats from him. I'll have to go pantyless since he destroyed last night's pair, but luckily, I have spares in my locker at the station. Finding my bra, I put it on, followed by the offered sweats and a LFFD tee that I pick up off the floor.

Tying it in a knot at the side, since it's three sizes too big, I look up and see Kip gazing at me. "What?" I self-consciously ask.

"I stand corrected, you are sexy as hell in my clothes too. I think you could even make a potato sack look sexy."

"We can try out your theory another time, right now, we need to head to the station and help out."

"After you," he says, and together we make our way to the firehouse.

In the distance, I see the smoke billowing into the air, and a feeling of unease washes over me the closer we get to the firehouse.

10

KIP

When we arrive at the station, the first truck is already at the scene, and the second truck is in the driveway, ready to depart. Our crew is in their seats and waiting for us. "Let's go, Kitson, Summers," Cap sings out as he climbs up into the front passenger seat.

Since I'm dressed appropriately, I pull on my fire suit while Tate rushes inside to change. A few moments later, she steps outside and she takes my breath away all over again. I wonder what it would be like to fuck her on the top of the truck? Or in the bunk rooms?

She slams the door shut and settles into the seat next to me, bumping my shoulder. Dropping my gaze to hers, I smile when I see her grinning back at me.

She winks but at the sound of her dad's voice, she turns her attention to him and focuses on what he's saying.

A warehouse downtown has caught fire, and it's rapidly spread to the adjoining buildings, one of which happens to be a chemical factory. The flames are yet to reach the chemical factory but fire has a mind of its own and is extremely unpredictable. The contents inside that factory are highly volatile, and it's imperative we get the blaze under control quickly. Otherwise, we're risking an explosion and mass casualties. As it stands now, no one has been hurt. We'd like to keep it that way.

We arrive downtown and the fire is blazing. Fire is so pretty to look at but at the same time, it's destructive and doesn't care what's in its way. It doesn't discriminate and will engulf anything and everything in its path to feed the flames.

The truck comes to a stop, and we all climb out, falling into line and starting our allocated tasks. I love working with this crew; we all know what we need to do, and we do it without complaint. Like a well-oiled machine, we do what we're trained to do, and five grueling hours later, the fire is extinguished with no injuries.

We had to call in teams from nearby for assistance

but we did it, the flames are out and no one was injured. All that's left of the warehouse is ash, broken beams, and a devastated owner. The fire was a raging inferno, and it almost demolished everything in its path. We managed to save the surrounding warehouses, including the chemical one, and in the process, we prevented a major catastrophe from occuring.

Before we leave, we need to do one more check on the building to ensure there are no embers still burning and make sure that no one is inside. In teams of two, we each take a section and do our checks. I'm paired with Kain, and we've been assigned to the second floor of the three-story building. Tate and Marcus have been given the top floor.

We make our way inside, being careful to not fall through the floor or disturb any of the structural beams. Even though they are metal, the fire was intense, and we don't know what it did to the integrity of them. Luckily for us, the fire protection around the metal seems to be intact so we shouldn't have any issues.

"So, you and my sister, huh?" Kain says as we clear the first room we inspect.

"Well, you did say to go for it."

"Yeah, but I didn't think you'd act so quickly."

"Did you see how hot she was last night? I wasn't going to bide my time and let some other fucker swoop in and get the girl."

"You sound whipped already."

"I think you might be right. Kain, your sister is fucking amazing and the things she does with her tong—"

"Lalalalalalalalala," he singsongs, covering his ears. "I'm happy you're both happy but I do not, I repeat, *do not* need you to finish that sentence ... or start any sentences about what happens behind closed doors."

I nod at him. "Duly noted." Almost as soon as the words leave my mouth, the floor above collapses. A feminine scream ricochets throughout the area, followed by the sound of everything crashing to the floor behind us. "Fuck," I screech as we race toward the debris.

"Keep back!" Kain shouts. I know he's right, I need to stop and assess. Turning to face him, I nod in understanding but before I can reply, there's an explosion below us, and the floorboards beneath my feet give way and suddenly I'm weightless. I'm floating through the air and falling to the level below. Wood, ash, and floorboards fill the air around me, and with a thud, I land on the cement floor—my head cracks against it.

Lying on my back, I stare up at the sky above, the wind knocked out of me. Blinking rapidly, I take stock of my body and sigh in relief when nothing feels broken, and I can wiggle my toes. Toe wiggling is always a good sign after falling one story onto your back.

A noise nearby garners my attention so I turn my head and squint. The air is thick with ash and smoke but from the corner of my eye, I see orange and yellow flames flickering amongst the darkness. "Shit, shit, shit," I mumble to myself.

Pushing myself up, I radio that I'm okay. I don't get a response. I'm fairly certain I damaged it in the fall. Turning around in circles, I look for the exit, and that's when I see Tate trapped under a pile of debris. She was up on the third floor before disaster struck, her now being on the ground floor is bad, really really bad. "Tate!" I cry out, and as I make my way over to her, another explosion rocks through the room. Once again, I'm flying through the air, and I hit something hard. Dropping to the concrete floor, the last thing I see before darkness takes me is Tate's lifeless body and flames billowing around us.

11

TATUM

ONE MINUTE I'M WALKING ALONG THE BACK wall, gazing at the mountains in the distance, listening to Marcus tell me about his night with one of the bar staff from The James Hotel, and the next I'm falling through the floor. A scream slips from my lips and then a groan when I crash down on the second level. The roof above gave way, and when it came down, it took me and the flooring beneath me with it. Somehow nothing is crushing me and thankfully, I can move my toes.

Someone nearby yells "Get back!" The voice is familiar, but there's a ringing in my ears, and my vision is blurry. I can't focus clearly. Then there's an explosion and the floor beneath me gives way. Once again, I'm falling. However, this time when I land,

I'm not so lucky. Something lands on my arm, and I hear a snap while something heavy pins my legs down. When I try to wiggle my toes, I can't. Panic begins to filter through me; like a shot of heroine, it seeps through my body. That fear begins to increase when I see flames in the distance. My breathing becomes ragged, and I begin to hyperventilate.

Closing my eyes, I focus on my breathing.

Inhale.

Exhale.

Repeat.

But it's not working. It's becoming harder and harder to breathe. No matter how much I inhale, exhale, repeat, I can't control my breathing. The room starts to fill with smoke, and that isn't helping either. My vision begins to dot due to lack of oxygen. My eyelids are heavy; it's like they are weighted down.

Someone yells my name, and the sound of the familiar voice causes me to open my eyes. From my trapped position, I can't see where they are. That doesn't matter, though, because there's another explosion.

A heat like I've never felt before flies past me, engulfing the room. I'm thankful to be trapped under this metal sheet because it saves me from being burned alive, but it's hotter than Hades right now. My heart is racing and fear like never before envelops me. "Heeeeeelllp!" I shout out but with the sound of the roaring flames, no one can hear me.

I'm lying here trapped, about to burn to death, but I smile when I think about last night and this morning with Kip. At least I had one last happy moment before I die. "I'm sorry, Kip," I whisper as the heat becomes too much, and I pass out.

12

KIP

"WHAT ARE YOU DOING OUT OF BED?" CAP ASKS me as I pace back and forth in front of the nurses' desk, waiting for news on Tatum. My head is throbbing from the concussion, and my chest hurts from inhaling nasty fumes after the second explosion. And my heart, well, it's breaking into a million tiny pieces because the woman I'm falling in love with is currently in surgery. The doctors are resetting her broken wrist, and on top of that, she hasn't regained consciousness since she was pulled from the rubble.

When my eyes landed on her amongst the debris, it felt like the floor let go again. I failed her. I didn't reach her before the second explosion, and now ... now she's badly injured and there's nothing I can do.

This waiting and not being able to do anything is frustrating.

"Kip," Cap growls again. "You'll be no good to Tate if you're dead on your feet. Now go back to your room and rest."

"But—" He raises his hand, stopping me from protesting further, and even though I know I need to look after me, I need to be here for Tate.

"No *buts*, Kip. I don't need any more of my crew in surgery. Now, turn around and go back to your room. As soon as I have an update, I'll let you know."

"I can't lose her," I tell him.

Lowering my head, I close my eyes, and a vision of her riding me earlier this morning flashes before my eyes. What if that was our only time together? What if I don't get a chance with her? What if. What if. What if. There's too many what-ifs right now, and I don't like the answer to any of them.

"And you won't. My daughter is a fighter, Kip. She won't let a three-story fall through a burning building knock her down."

He somehow makes me chuckle with that comment, and the sound of my laugher screeches through my brain, making me squint in pain. Deep down, I know he's right. Tate may be the most beautiful woman on both the inside and the outside but she's also tough as nails. She's the only chick at the firehouse, and even though she's the captain's daughter, she doesn't take any nepotism from him—not that he's inclined that way—or shit from us. She gives as good as she gets, and if anything, she's rougher than us guys. That only adds to the amazingness that is Tatum Summers.

"Kip Kitson," Ginny berates from behind me. "What are you doing out of bed? And, Shaun Summers, why did you not march him back to his room? He has a concussion and fell through the floor of a burning warehouse."

"I tried ... but he's stubborn ... like your daughter."

"And that stubbornness is what will pull her through this," she matter-of-factly states to Shaun, then she looks to me. "Bed. Now, mister."

"Fine," I relent. She takes my arm, and together we shuffle down the hallway to my room. When we reach my room, I'm met with an irate nurse.

"You, sir, are meant to be resting and on oxygen to help your lungs. Do I need to sedate and intubate you? Because I will. I know you care about your friend but if you're not breathing, you won't be able to help her with her recovery."

"Fine," I hiss through clenched teeth.

Climbing back into bed, Ginny fusses with the blankets while the cranky nurse reattaches the finger pulse thingy and the nose tube. She's less than gentle with me but I probably deserve it. I'm being a cranky fucker right now, and she's just trying to do her job, but I can't stop worrying about Tate. As if Ginny is in my mind, she takes my hand in hers. "She'll be fine, Kip," she says, her voice laced with determination.

"How can you be so confident?" I ask her.

"It's a mom thing. I can't explain it, but I just know that she'll be fine."

"I hope you're right."

"I am ... and I cannot wait to see you two fall in love."

Her words cause me to smile. "You really think she'll fall in love with me?"

"I know so, it's another mom thing. Now, you get some rest and get your strength up. Tatum is going to need you when she gets out of here."

With one final squeeze of my hand, Ginny leaves my room, and I realize she's right. I'd know if Tate was gone. My heart hurts right now but that's from the accident, not the loss of Tate. Closing my eyes, I drift off to sleep and dream of a happy life with Tate.

13

TATUM

THERE'S AN INCESSANT BEEPING, AND IT'S grinding through my brain. My body feels numb and heavy, but at the same time I feel like I'm floating. I try to open my eyes but I can't. There's a muffled sound amongst the beeping, and then I hear a soft voice. "I can't lose her, Shaun, I can't lose my baby girl."

"Mom?" I say but it echoes and I realize, I internally said it.

There's a pressure on my hand, and what feels like a kiss on my knuckles. "Please wake up, baby, we've only just begun our journey."

"Kip?" I say his name like a question but again, it's only in my head.

I'm so confused right now. I can hear but I can't

reply, it's like I'm stuck inside my head floating between consciousness and sleep. There's a pressure on my hand and it calms me. I want to squeeze it back but I can't. I try with all my might to squeeze back, but nothing. I try to wriggle my toes, and I think I am but I'm not sure. It's an odd feeling to not have control of your body. It's like I'm here but not, and I don't like it. I don't like it at all.

"Please, baby, wake up. Don't leave me," Kip pleads and his words give me a boost but as much as I try, I can't move or reply.

"You need to get some rest, son." That sounds like Dad.

"I'm not going anywhere. I'm not leaving this room until I see her beautiful green eyes staring up at me. I don't want her to wake up alone."

"Kip," Dad says in his *I mean business* voice. "As I keep saying, you're no good to her if you're dead on your feet. You were also injured."

"I'm fine," Kip snaps at Dad.

"A concussion is not fine," Dad growls out.

"Shaun," Mom pleads with Dad. "Leave the boy alone. He's fine here by her side, he has us to watch over him and access to medical help if something happens."

"He has medical help and a perfectly good room

just down the hall," I hear Dad say, and I'm sure he's shaking his head in frustration right now. Mom will be holding on to his upper arm and resting her head on his shoulder. I hate that I'm putting everyone through this, but no matter how hard I try, I can't will my eyes open. I try to wriggle my toes again but like earlier, I can't even do that. I can't do anything but lie here and listen to those I love fall apart around me.

I keep trying to wriggle my toes and suddenly a feeling of dread washes over me. I can't feel my toes, that's not a good sign and of all the shit I'm in, that scares me the most. I keep trying to wriggle them but it's taking all the energy I have, and I start to get sleepy again.

"You wake up now, Tatum Prudence Summers," Mom says and I hear someone laugh.

"You just got middle named and you can't even defend yourself," Kain teases, mentally I flip him the bird, asshole has always teased me over my middle name. Mind you, he's one to talk, his middle *names*, plural, are Abner Alaric.

"Kain Abner Alaric Summers, leave your sister alone," Mom hisses.

Suck on that, Brozart, I think to myself.

Exhaustion is creeping in but I don't want to succumb to it. I want to hold on to this sliver of reality for as long as I can, but my body has other ideas and I once again drift off into darkness.

That beeping noise is back again but rather than it reverberating through my brain like the last time I woke, well subconsciously woke, it's loud and vibrates through my body. My body that I can feel. A body that no longer feels like it's floating. I try to wriggle my toes, and this time, they move. My toes move. "I can wriggle my toes," I whisper and when I hear the words out loud rather than it echoing in my head, my eyes fly open, but I quickly scrunch them shut again due to the brightness of the room.

"Tate, babe," Kip says, his voice full of hope. "Please open your eyes again." I try to open them again but it feels like they're glued shut.

"No. No. No," I plead with myself, just as Kip begs, "Please, Baby, wake up. I miss you and need to see your beautiful eyes."

With everything I have, I concentrate on opening my eyes. After what feels like forever, I open them and they stay open. The room is just as bright but it's not as stabby stabby on my eyes and skull this time. Everything is blurry. I rapidly blink and the brightness dims as the room comes into focus. The first thing I see is Kip, there's a bandage wrapped around his head and his green eyes are bloodshot, puffy, and red.

"I'm here," I cry. My eyes welling with tears. "I'm here," I whisper. Lifting my hand, I cup his cheek in my palm.

"Thank fuck, I was so worried." He leans forward and presses his lips to mine. The first tear falls and it's followed by an avalanche of them. "Don't you ever scare me like that again."

"I'll try," I murmur against his lips.

A noise by the door causes him to pull back, and I immediately feel the loss of him, but at the same time, I can breathe easily. Kissing him was worth the breathlessness. He looks over his shoulder and I can tell he's smiling. "She's awake," he excitedly says and when he turns back to me, I realize I was right. He is grinning from ear to ear and then I find myself doing the same, when over his shoulder my gaze lands on Mom, Dad, and Kain standing there. Seeing them causes me to cry again, crying hurts my head right now but I can't stop the tears.

When I woke earlier and they couldn't hear me and I couldn't move my toes, I thought the worst, but seeing and hearing them is such a relief, and I continue to let that relief pour out of my eyes and down my cheeks.

Mom comes over and half hugs me. I go to lift my arms to hug her back, and that's when I realize that one of my arms is covered in a purple cast, and the other has a drip attached to it. "I'm so glad you're awake, Tatum. Don't you ever scare me like that again."

"I promise, Mom."

"Let me at her," Dad growls from behind Mom. She kisses my forehead and moves aside for Dad to have his turn. He leans down and hugs me. "Can you wiggle your toes?"

"Yes, Dad, I can."

"Show me," he demands. He pulls the blanket covering me back and when he sees me wriggling my toes, he nods. "Good, good." He looks at me again. "Ohh, by the way, you're fired. I can't go through that again."

"Like fuck I'm fired!" I shout at him, squinting when the shrillness of my voice vibrates through my brain.

"Language, lady," he sneers.

"Well, don't fire me and I won't swear."

"Tatum, you nearl—"

"Shaun," Mom interrupts. "This is not the time

to discuss this. Let's just focus on the fact that she's awake and can wriggle her toes."

"But—"

"Not buts, Shaun Summers." Mom's sternness causes me to giggle but then she turns and focuses on me. My smile drops and the giggle gets stuck in my throat when I see the look on her face. "And the same goes for you, missy. You need to focus on getting better. Work will still be there."

"Yes, Mom," I say, just as Dad grumbles, "Fine ... lucky I love you, woman."

Dad walks over to the bed, tugs Mom away from me, and pulls her into his arms before kissing her on the side of her head.

I find myself grinning as I watch them, and then I focus on Kip. He smiles at me but it doesn't reach his eyes, seeing him like that causes me to worry. "Are you okay? What's with the ninja bandage?"

"I have a concussion," he informs me.

"Why are you not resting? You need to look after you," I admonish him.

"I'm fine, I just need to rest and now that I know you're awake, I can."

"And sitting in an uncomfortable, shit green hospital chair at my bedside is resting?"

"It's not shit green," he throws back at me.

"But it's uncomfortable. Here," I offer and shimmy over, giving him room to slide in next to me. He just sits there, flicking his gaze from the mattress to me and back. "Get in the bed, Kitson," I growl at him.

"I see bossy Tater-Tot is still with us," Kain teases me, earning himself a purple wrist covered bird flip. "Yep, I was correct."

"Shut it, Brozart."

"One of these days, you two need to tell me how these nicknames came about."

"Sure," I reply. While Kain hisses at the same time, "Not a fucking chance."

"Language, Kain Summers," Dad berates him.

"Har har, you got in trouble."

"Taaaaate," Dad warns me, adding five extra a's in my name.

"Har har, you got in trouble," Kain singsongs, earning himself a smack upside the head. "Ugh, Dad, what the hell?"

"Language, I won't tell you again. And stop taunting your sister, she's in the hospital."

"I was too, you know," he hisses and crosses his arms defensively.

"What happened? Are you okay?" I ask him.

"Just a precaution to be checked out in the ER

since I was thrown in the blast, I was still on the second floor so it wasn't as bad as you two." He pauses, "Looks like you two have fallen—literally—for each other."

"Kain, that was such a bad pun." I turn to Kip. "But yeah, I think I am, literally and figuratively."

"My heart only beats for you," he whispers and presses a kiss to the side of my head.

"My heart only beats for you, too."

A sniff from Mom causes me to start to blush while Kain stands there and fake gags, earning himself another smack upside the head from Dad. I cannot believe my parents and brother just heard Kip and I confess our true feelings for one another. It's too soon to love him but one day I think I will. For now though, my heart only beats for him, and it will do so until my last dying breath.

14

KIP

...ten months later

I'M LIVING THE DREAM LIFE RIGHT NOW. LIFE here in Lockhart Falls is perfect. I have an amazing job, great friends, and a sexy as hell girlfriend. Yep. Tatum Summers is officially my girlfriend. After us confessing how we felt about each other while she was in the hospital, we made it official and the day she was discharged, I asked her an important question ...

    ... *I'm sitting in my Jeep, staring at the hospital building. Tate is being discharged today and the relief at knowing she has no lasting damage is so fucking good to know. I still feel guilty that I didn't get to her in time, but no one could have. Superman, maybe, but*

I'm man enough to admit that I'm not Superman. I'm a super man, two words, but I'm not the dude in a blue cape.

I'm shitting bricks right now because I'm going to ask her an important question today, and I really hope she says yes. I have never been this nervous at the prospect of asking a question, but this is a super important one. I probably should have asked her parents first, but when I woke up this morning, I thought about the morning after the ball and well, now I can't stop thinking about waking up next to her every day.

A knock on my car window frightens me, and when I look up, I see Tate's mom and dad. Climbing out of my car, I greet them. "Morning, Cap. Ginny. How are you both today?"

"Happy to have my baby girl coming home today," Ginny excitedly says.

"Yeah, I'll be glad to not visit this place anymore. I hate that hospital smell."

"Let's hope we don't have to come back here anytime soon." She squeezes my forearm and smiles up at me.

"Amen to that." We all fall silent, then I begin to wonder if maybe they just want family to be here.

Shuffling, I bite my lip. "Is it okay that I'm here today? Or do you want it to be just family?"

"You are family, Kip," Ginny says, once again squeezing my forearm in the way that I presume a loving mom would to reiterate their point.

"As long as you're sure? I don't want to overstep."

"Kip," Cap rumbles. "You've been here every day since the fire. If you don't come in with us, Tate will be devastated and that's the last thing we want. You've been a part of our lives since you arrived here two months ago and now that you're her boyfriend, that makes you family in my eyes."

"Thanks, Cap. I ... I've never had a family before so this means the world to me. Your daughter means the world to me."

"Good," he growls. "Because you hurt her, and well, you'll be down under, and I'm not referring to the kangaroo land you hail from."

A laugh slips out. "Kain said something similar the night of the ball when I saw Tate naked."

"What?" he hisses.

"Ummm, ahhh, shitballs. Can we forget this conversation happened and go get Tate?"

"That sounds lovely." Ginny nods in agreement. "Come on, Shaun, let's go."

Mouthing thank you to Ginny for saving my ass just now, the three of us walk into the hospital and the closer to Tate's room we get, the more nervous I become. We smile at the nurses at the desk when we walk past. One of the nurses asks to speak with her parents, so I continue to her room. When I walk in and see her, I swear my heart skips a beat. My girlfriend—I kinda love saying that—is standing at the window, gazing at the mountains surrounding the Lockhart Falls hospital. She's wearing a black and white spotted sundress, her hair is hanging in loose waves down her back, and the only indication that she was nearly blown up eleven days ago is the purple cast on her arm and a few fading bruises on her back. She was so fucking lucky she wasn't killed.

As if she senses me, she spins around to face me. With the morning light beaming through the window, she looks like an angel and I tell her so. "You, Tatum Summers, look like an angel."

"You, Kip Kitson, need your eyes checked but thanks for telling me a lie."

"It's not a lie when it's the truth but I, ummm, ahh, I need to ask you something."

"You can ask me anything."

Nodding my head, I walk over to her, I take her hands in mine, and I stare into green eyes that are eerily like mine. "Move in with me?"

"Huh?" she deadpans.

"When you leave here today, don't go home to your parents' place, come home with me. Move in with me."

"You want me to move in?"

"Yep, it's fucking crazy, but you make me crazy in the bestest of ways. When I woke up this morning, I thought about the morning after the ball. Waking up with you next to me was the best feeling in the world, and I know it's fucking crazy to be asking since we've only been dating for a week and a bit and you've been in the hospital all that time and I still need to take you out on a first date but you're it for me, Tate and I want to spend every moment with you."

She moves her head up and down, processing my words. Her mouth opens and closes but nothing comes out, and I begin to wonder if I came on too strong but then she whispers one word, "Okay."

"Okay you'll move in with me, okay? Or you're fucking crazy, Kip, okay? I need you to clarify which okay you mean."

A smile graces her face and she begins to nod quickly. "Okay, I'll move in with you. This is crazy as all hell but, Kip, I have never felt like this with anyone before. I've had time to think while I've been here, and I don't want to let life slip by with what-ifs.

I'm going to jump and take risks and moving in with you is a risk I'm willing to take."

"Really?"

"Really, really ... but you need to tell Daddy."

"Tell Daddy what?" Cap says from the doorway.

Spinning around, I stare at Cap and Ginny. "I ... ummm." Crap, I'm so nervous. "I—"

"We're moving in together," Tate shouts from next to me.

"Looks like you owe me a spa weekend," Ginny says to Cap.

"You made another bet?" Tate hisses, shaking her head at her parents.

"We told you; we make bets all the time," her mom nonchalantly replies.

"I think I've missed something." *I'm confused right now but the three of them seem to know something I don't.*

"I'll fill you in when we get home."

Home, I love hearing her say that, and one day, I'm going to marry this woman. She makes my heart full, and for the first time in my life, I'm happy and content.

Eight months later, our love is still burning hot; in and out of the bedroom but it's more than that. Tatum and I connect on every level. She's the peanut butter to my honey ... yes, my Aussie is showing but peanut butter and honey is the ducks nuts, and I will say so until I die. And for the record, PB&J sucks and is disgusting.

The only downside? My time here is coming to an end. In two months' time I'll be returning to Australia and to life back in Bauckle Beach. I don't know how I feel about that. I miss Australia so much, but the thought of leaving Tate guts me. It absolutely guts me.

I've found "the one." I know it's only been a short period of time, but when you know, you know, and Tatum Prudence Summers is it for me. My heart only beats for her, and it will continue to do so for the rest of my life. Proving that we're meant to be, later that night, Tate confirms that we're meant to be in the most epic of ways.

15

TATUM

"Ohhh, Tatum, I'm so excited for you," Mom says, wiping a tear from her eye as she looks over my surprise for Kip.

"Mom, don't you start crying 'cause then I'll start crying, and I'll be one big snot-faced, teary mess, and that's not how I want to look when I do this."

"But you'd be a beautiful snot-faced, teary mess and, can I just say, thank you for winning me another spa weekend." Tonight I'm going to do something crazy, but ever since the idea popped into my head last week, I haven't been able to stop thinking about it. I ran the idea past Mom, and before I'd even finished, she was beaming with excitement and I just knew, they'd made another bet.

"You and Dad bet again, didn't you?"

"Yep." She nods with a big grin. "I said this would happen. He wasn't convinced but I know my daughter."

Shaking my head, I take it back from Mom and slip it into my handbag. "Well, I better get going, I want to make chicken parmigiana, homemade French fries, and salad to go along with this surprise." Personally, I prefer pasta with a parmigiana, but Kip's an Aussie and they do so many weird things down under that I will make it the Aussie way, just for him.

"He'll definitely say yes then." Kip introduced us to the Aussie version of chicken parmigiana or a parma, as the Aussies like to call it. It's a staple in our house, and we eat it at least once a month. And I mean, what's not to love about fried chicken, tomato sauce, ham, and cheese?

"You always told me that the way to a man's heart is through his stomach."

"This is true. After all, it was my mac and cheese that won your father over all those years ago."

"That's 'cause your mac and cheese is *da bomb*."

"Thanks, Sweetie, and your parmi is pretty amazing too."

"It's a parma, Mom," I state matter-of-factly, earning myself an eye roll and a shake of the head from Mom. Apparently that's a running argument in Australia, you're either Team Parma or Team Parmi ... and so it seems, this debate occurs in the Summers's household too. FYI, the correct term is parma. "And we both know that Kip's is better than mine."

"I think they're both divine. Now, you better get going. You have a *parmI*"—she emphasizes the I at the end—"to make but please, for the love of God, text me later and let me know how it all goes."

"Will do, Mom." I smile at her.

"I'm one-billion percent confident that it's going to play out like you're hoping, I feel it in my bones."

"Me too, Mom, me too. I'm not even a little bit nervous so I know it's meant to be."

Kissing Mom on the cheek, I hug and tell her goodbye. Heading out to my car, I climb in and drive to the store to grab what I need for my parma dinner. With the ingredients and a bottle of champagne in hand, I make my way to the cashier and then head home.

It's still surreal that Kip and I are living together. We haven't even been dating for a year but it's been perfect in every way. When you find the one you love, time doesn't mean anything. It's just a number;

but he's my number one, and I cannot wait for my surprise tonight.

I've just popped the parmigiana's into the oven, so I race through the bedroom and into the en suite. I quickly shave my legs and the important bits before jumping into the shower. I slip into a purple halter dress; it's a little dressier than what I would normally wear at home, but I want tonight to be perfect. I mean, it's not every day a girl does this, and suddenly, this girl has become really nervous.

"Honey, I'm home," Kip sings out from the other room, and hearing his voice instantly calms me. With three words, those nerves disappear, and that reconfirms to me that this is meant to be.

Walking out to greet him, I smile when I see him in a pair of black cargo pants and a LFFD T-shirt. "Hey, handsome," I say in greeting.

"Hey hey, pretty lady." He slides his arm around my waist and pulls me in for a kiss. Like most welcome home kisses between us, it turns heated and in the blink of an eye, I'm bent over the arm of the sofa and he's fucking me from behind.

It's hard.

It's fast.

It's amazing.

It's us to a T.

"That was unexpected," he says as he pulls his pants back up, and I readjust my panties and dress.

"Really? That was unexpected? I think we *hello fuck* like that at least three times a week."

"Well, yeah, have you seen you? You look fucking hot tonight, are we celebrating something?"

"Umm ... well, ahh ... we need to talk."

"Shit, that statement is never followed by good news." He runs his hand through his hair. "Was that a goodbye fuck just now?"

"What?" I hiss, "No, that was our usual welcome home, it's Tuesday fuck."

"But it's Friday."

"Tuesday, Friday, whatever." I begin to pace back and forth, this isn't going how I expected it to go. "I look, I ... shit, can you just, fuck, why can't I get the words out."

Kip walks over to me, slides his arms around my waist and stares into my eyes. "Just tell me and then together we can come up with a game plan. It's you and me against the world, remember?"

Nodding, I smile at him. With just a few words, he's calmed me, and now I know I can do this. Pulling out of his embrace, I walk over to the table and pick up what I want to give him. Walking back over to him, I take his hand in mine and walk over to the sofa. Pushing him down, I sit next to him, and then I drop to one knee. Taking a deep breath, I turn his hand over and place the tickets in his palms. "Kip Kitson, will you travel the world with me before we move to Australia together?"

His eyes widen. "You ... you want to move home with me?"

"Yep." I nod. "I want to spend every waking moment with you, Kip. I love you more than peanut butter and honey. Wherever you go, I go. So, what do you say? We travel for a few months and then move to Bauckle Beach together?"

"Yes," he shouts, dropping to the floor in front of me. He grips my cheeks, the tickets scrunched in his hand. "I want to do that with you. I want to do everything with you. As long as you're by my side, I'm happy. And I too, love you more than peanut butter and honey. I love you to the moon and back times infinity-billion."

My smile widens at his words. "Infinity-billion, huh?" He nods. "Well, I love you infinity-billion plus one."

He chuckles at my one up and the smile on his face is brighter than the sun shining on a hot summer's—pun kinda intended—day. He leans forward and kisses me. This kiss reminds me of our first one at the annual firefighter's ball earlier this year. That was the night my heart started beating differently, it started to beat for Kip and Kip only, well me too because well, I need my heart pumping to live. My heart filled with love that night and now that I have Kip in my life, I'm never letting him go. One day I'll become Mrs. Kitson but for now, I'm content being Tatum Summers ... who's moving to Australia with her hunky Aussie firefighter.

EPILOGUE
KIP

...three years later

FLOPPING ONTO MY BACK, I STARE UP AT THE ceiling, panting and completely spent. My heart is racing after making love to my fiancée, yep, Tate and I are engaged. I slapped a ring on that, and soon she will officially be mine forever. She snuggles into my side, and throwing her leg over mine, she absent-mindedly runs her fingertips through the hair on my chest. Resting her hand over my heart she murmurs, "I love you, Kip Kitson."

"And I love you, Tatum Prudence Summers." Smiling, I place a kiss on her head and wait for it.

"Ugh, you had to middle name me?"

"Yep, sure did."

"You're lucky I love you, Kitson."

"Hell yeah, I am. The day you agreed to marry me was the happiest day of my life."

"I thought the happiest day was when you attended your first fire?"

"It was ... until you said yes, that is."

"Aww, you're too sweet."

"I know," I cockily reply.

"Modest, too."

"Yet you still love me." She digs me in the ribs. "Hey, that hurt."

"Aww, does the big, bad firefighter want me to kiss it better?"

Placing my finger under her chin, I lift until her eyes are on mine. I stare into her gorgeous green orbs and wink. "I know something else you can kiss." Raising my eyes suggestively, I gently run my palm down her side and across her stomach. With my eyes still locked on hers, I circle her navel before ever so slowly sliding my fingertip toward her pussy. She rolls to her back and widens her legs for me. She raises her eyebrows suggestively back at me, the minx. So, I turn the path of my fingers around and head back up her stomach. She growls and I laugh. She opens her mouth to speak but before she can utter a word, I cup her mound with my palm. I apply pressure to her clit before slipping my middle finger into her wet folds. I'm not sure if she's turned on from this or if its remnants from our lovemaking only moments ago. With my eyes locked on hers, I pump my finger in and out. Adding a second digit, I slow down my ministrations. Leaning forward, I press my lips to hers as my tongue slides into her mouth in sync with my fingers in her pussy.

Her walls clench around my fingers, and she screams her release into my mouth. She's still coming down from her orgasm when I lift her onto my lap. Lifting to her knees, she slides down my cock and begins to rock her hips in circles. Lifting her hands, she fondles her breasts. Not wanting to miss out, I lift my hands, and together, we massage her tits; I tug on her nipples until they are stiff peaks.

Sitting up, I hold her to my chest, and she wraps her legs around my waist. I piston my hips up as she thrusts down. I bury my face in her tits and lick her skin. Taking a nipple into my mouth, I gently bite down. She moans and the sound resonates in my balls and they begin to tingle. Tatum reaches behind her and squeezes them. "Babe, if you do that again, I'm going to explode before you do."

"That's okay."

"No, it's not," I growl through clenched teeth,

leaning forward I suck her nipple harder, garnering a guttural growl from her. Sliding my hand between us, I press down on her clit. Her head drops back and another deep moan slips from her lips. Her walls clench my cock and she grunts—she's coming. The sound sets me off, and together, we ride out our climax.

Tatum lifts her head and gazes into my eyes. I feel the love radiating from her with that one look. Our moment is interrupted when my phone pings with the station's alert tone. Soon after, Tatum's beeps too. We look quizzically at each other.

Reaching over, I grab my beeping phone and read the message. "Shit," I mumble. "This is bad, epically bad."

THE END!

To find out if it was epically bad, you can see what happens in *After the Ashes*.

To find out what happens next for Tatum, you can in After the Ashes.

Available to buy now!

ASHES
ASHES

P L CALLIE

I never pictured a life without Kip. It was supposed to be me and him until the end, but the universe always has a way of screwing things up.

Moving on after losing him wasn't something I thought I was capable of, but when Penn Brookes comes into the picture, I realize I'm not so alone.

Suffering the same kind of loss as me and trying to be the best dad he can, I start to gravitate toward him.

We're one in the same, building our lives around broken pieces, and suddenly, something I never thought possible happens.

That spark I've only felt once before returns and lights something deep inside me.

Can we overcome our grief and build something great, or will the circumstances of the past stand in the way?

ACKNOWLEDGMENTS

These things never get any easier and I always feel like I've forgotten someone so this is a blanket thank you to everyone who I have crossed paths with on this authoring journey.

Karen Hrdlicka from **Barren Acres Editing**; thank you for everything that you do for me.

Tori, Margaret and **Lana;** thank you for checking all my I's are dotted, my T's are crossed and there's no extra e's or s's.

Amanda thank you for the cover. I first fell in love with the one for After the Ashes and then when this story came, you once again nailed the cover.

My beta babes **Bec, Margaret, Sarah** and **Tara;** I would be lost without you ladies. You give me advice when I second guess everything and you helped to bring this story to life. Thank you from the bottom of my heart...and I'm sorry for what's about to happen in Ashes to Ashes **insert angel face**

Troy, my husband, my everything. You really are awesome at what you do and you're an even better husband and father. Love you long-time dude.

To my munchkins, **Piper** and **Kade**. You two are my greatest achievement and I'm so lucky to have you both in my life. Love you long-time guys and I look forward to the day when you are forty and can finally read my books.

And finally, **you, my reader**. This book is a different genre for me but I have to say, its one of my favs and I hope that you loved Chelsea and Kallen as much as I do.

Cheers,

Dana XoXoX

ALSO BY DL GALLIE

STAND ALONES

Antecedent

Doc Steel

Oops

Off the Books

Fractured: A driven world novel

Deck...the Balls

Secrets and Sunrises

Always in the Cards

Out of Nowhere

Before the Ashes

After the Ashes

Love Me Like You Do

Never Let Me Go

Seven Nights

Seven Kisses

PUCKING NOVELS

I Pucking Hate That I Love You

A Pucking Good Christmas

...and a few pucking more

FALLING NOVELS

These men make it hard not to fall for them

Falling for Dr. Kelly

Falling for Dr. Knight

Falling for Agent Cox

Falling for Agent Cruz

Falling: The Complete Collection

LORDS OF CRESTWOOD PREP

Co-write with Tara Lee

Thatcher

Reign

Hendrix

Saint

THE UNEXPECTED SERIES

When it comes to love, expect the unexpected

The Unexpected Gift

The Unexpected Letter

The Unexpected Package

The Unexpected Connection

The Unexpected series: The Complete Collection

THE CASTAWAY GROVE COLLECTION

Love has arrived in the Grove

Oasis

Unequivocal Love

Five Words

Broken Rules

...and a few more to come.

The Castaway Grove Collection, Vol 1

THE LIQUOR CABINET SERIES

Liquor has never been so disturbingly saucy

Malt Me (Book 1)

Tequila Healing (Book 2)

Wine Not (Book 3)

The Final Shot (Book 4)

The Liquor Cabinet: Series boxset

All of these books are available on Amazon.

FACEBOOK ~ INSTAGRAM ~ BOOKBUB

GOODREADS ~ WEBSITE

dlgallieauthor@outlook.com

Sign up to my newsletter

ABOUT THE AUTHOR

DL Gallie is from Queensland, Australia, but she's lived in many different places all over the world, including the UK and Canada. She currently resides in Central Queensland with her husband and two munchkins. She and her husband have been together since she was sixteen, and although they drive each other crazy at times, she couldn't imagine her life without him.

Shortly after her son was born, DL began reading again. With encouragement from her husband, she picked up the pen and started writing, and now the voices in her head won't shut up.

DL enjoys listening to music, drinking white wine in the summer, red wine in the winter, and beer all year round. She's also never been known to turn down a cocktail, especially a margarita.